HERBERT SANTORI

Mad Director's Cut

GUTENBERG WHITES

... 50 Years Too Late!

This is a work of fiction. Similarities to real people, places, or events are entirely coincidental.

GUTENBERG WHITES

First edition. January 31, 2023.

Copyright © 2023 Herbert Santori.

ISBN: 979-8215499542

Written by Herbert Santori.

Table of Contents

Gutenberg Whites 1

. ... 2

1 | POSTCARDS OF TIME... 10

2 | SILENCE OF SNOW 17

3 | THE TRAP 25

4 | RIVER FLOW 29

5 | DAWN 35

2020 | THE YEAR OF FEAR 49

6 | SWERVE, PAUSE, HIP 52

7 | OUR TOILET, PLANET EARTH 55

8 59

HERBERT SANTORI 67

Mad Director's Cut | GUTENBERG WHITES | ... 50 Years Too

Late! 68

PROFOUND SOUL DIGGER, PIRATE AND THE ETERNAL NOMAD,

STOPPING MEANS DYING AND OFF HE GOES.

FROM LANDING TO LANDING,

LAST INSTANCES ARE THE ONES THAT COUNT.

FOR REAL.

- Cinematographic Essay

How many prying eyes, through as many windows as places and even more postal addresses?

'Camera rolling, please.'

International, even, announcing – to declare something, always, *it's the fucking neighbour – quick, hide!*

Well, for Luigi Bosco none of this bothers him. No, the neighbour by the window is of another interpretation.

Autobiographical? As much as such, like salt and lemon on a wound and sometimes - but with Luigi Bosco everything is different: everyone changes in his presence, since Bosco travels over their souls; something he hadn't ordered – came by default.

Back in the studio, completely alone and apart from the cameraman, only Bosco, a lit cigarette and an ashtray listen to him. Plus the millions of souls scattered around the city and around the world, nowadays connected to the nanosecond – maybe Bosco will tell you about a future where nothing's like that, I don't know.

And a city that could be any other city or town. Made up of streets and pavements, dirty sidewalks - clean, residential areas, poor, rich – super rich; of neon lights and traffic lights oscillating between go, stop, start, stop, think twice – in these types of cities.

But, dressed up in a suit and tie, well presented and as far as possible, Bosco finds himself in the middle of a dilemma, there, sitting at the table of a television program.

From your television show where Bosco is the host.

A debate program. of hit and bait, the present.
News.

Old and new, while Bosco smokes, slowly – silence starting to border with deafening, the cameraman seems to think -, movement is asked, something must happen, Bosco knows!

Background of a huge screen in opaque black, two red lines just squaring it, no navy-blues, a studio in sober tones.

Serious.

While a wisp of smoke rises in the air, remembering the 70s, when people still smoked live.

Provocative?

Fire alarm about to go off, both camera and cameraman covered in raincoats, just in case, while Bosco finishes his cigarette, eyes focused on the viewers.

At home, while the camera zooms in.

Slowly.

While you think.

'Ladies and Gentleman, a very good evening. Snow fell and everything froze.'

Through abandoned cities, decomposing masks of a remote past not so distant, when everything collapsed around us in a world of pigs.

'We've abandoned the moral compass for half a dozen ducats,' continues Bosco, sadly unable to speak. Instead, Luigi Bosco speaks to you in his thoughts, in front of the camera.

And this moral compass that, well, for spiders, it rotates between *I don't give a shit, Maybe, Don't Even Think About It, Fake News, One Day, Maybe, If It's God's Will* and it rotates. It circles around, endlessly rotating in that moral compass of yours that no longer adds anything else other than lies to the plot.

Theory, plot and lie.

You were what you were and now you are not. You've become one of them, you're part of it – vassal of the algorithm.

You hid from a thousand truths so that your child could grow up healthy in a dirty world – and there's no turning back.

'Frame my face, Peter, slowly.'

Your son also grew up and had children.

He too hid them from the truths, and the snowball only got fat. Multiplied by the number of stars in the sky, squared, there you find yourself: with no solution, yet you continue, in that robotic being of yours.

In the inert whirl of forgotten passions – do you remember what *would you like to be when you grew up?*

Did you get there?

Yes or no it doesn't matter because here you are and there you are, now, inert human robot.

Background noise of an old crackling film, disturbing silence itself, gnawing the soul – yes, Luigi Bosco finds himself in a dilemma: not knowing what to say next, in front of the camera.

And thinks.

He looks right in the middle of the camera and thinks.

He thinks of his almost non-existent hair.

Bald.

For some people, getting fat adds something positive – a bit of mass gives them this healthy look, and Bosco is not one of them. Of attractive, just the greying beard and recently, he only had to wait half a century.

But Bosco had always been a robust, vivacious man - always straightforward, both in spirit and physique. Resolute. Nowadays known as Wild-Beard or Barba-Löca. That's what they called him and that's how it was, he himself adding those two dots on top of the *o* as though Nordic.

Two dots.
Snow tone.

Ö

Ring, circle of life – two eyes, antennae.
Instigation, king, queen, crown – tribal.
Dot-dot, ring, ring- ring, union, doom, dishonour, ruin – victory!

Infinite.

Eternal.

Eternal journey, meaning and to mean.

To be.
Exist.
What else do I see in an Ö?

'And what else is there to see? All white. All snow. The wolf beside me.'

We became two pillars, heavy yet mobile, wandering from region to region; because, made up of voices that hover in the air like ghosts, for Bosco this is a dilemma flying over half-elation, half-lies, future thoughts and ideas – or ideals: how to be, who to be, how to present yourself; what to say, before it blows up in your face; what to wear, as long as it's woven by some child, there, far away, in the third world.

Where nothing affects us.

Because you know nothing about it.

Until one day you know it but you don't. In the inertia of the robotic being you've become, with no ideal but yours – fuck all – the rubber of the tire that carries you on a daily basis, what do you know about chemistry? From the moment I transport you from one side to the other, fuck that Chinese and his putrefied lungs.

'In this kind of tone I'd like to speak on my show.'

They made us like this.

From the opaque black screen behind him, images jump out of everything Bosco thinks – the result of a long, very long editing – decades of archive, so to speak; decades of editing, all of this happening behind Bosco and on the screen – the transition of a century in images – *millennia!* - which now becomes what the viewer sees, you too, from the comfort of your home, slash phone: wars, politics, *coups d'état* – men with full moustaches – conspiracies, in black and white and in colour; Woman, modesty, shamelessness!

The inevitable train of progress in an advance of ideas to the present day, dressed to match.

Glamourised.

Orchestral clarinets of pomp and circumstance, historical event, one after another, the history of the thinker who accompanied the thinking. The reason for thinking – the thinkers and the indoctrination of thousands of eras, repressed and condensed in one: today and the next step.

Hard rock on soft stone...

Snow fell and everything froze.

Through the abandoned city, masks on the ground of a remote but not so distant past, when everything collapsed around us.

Seven decades later, the year is 2096 and there are no more flags – we broke the scale and started eating ourselves for lack of nutrition – the cannibal instinct was always there, very present and waiting.

And we didn't hesitate a big deal when push came to shove.

Snow fell and everything froze.

Prognosis?

Durable – neither wolf nor reindeer – 'Outdoor light, studio 1 to be turned off, please - Bosco in the dark.'

The bonfire had become a mixture of luxury and carnal decoy: if you light it up, you warm up, but not without ceasing to attract.

Human heat.

It's not enough.

It's soul-freezing.

No forgiveness – no sun or see for months. And those months that no one counts anymore – what year is it?

Scissors!

You can shave that crazy beard you've been carrying around for years.

Canned food, expired half-a-hundred years ago, and you can't even tell what year you're in; you've lost the comparative term – Spring and

Winter have become the same part of a whole – it's all the same, nothing changes and you know nothing.

All white.

Snow-white with purplish blue tones, sometimes of thistle flower.

Howls the wolf, outside in the village.

Abandoned village, which had become temporary home. From house to house, walking on authentic pillows of snow; decades of endless snow, searching for food, clothing and utensils that may allow you to continue.

Howls the wolf, outside, hungry.

You squeeze the rifle to your body, equipped with nothing more than air and rust, as if survival depended on shooting, but you know well that, in the end, it will have to be *mano-a-mano*.

Counts seconds.

You see the wolf sniffing at you through the window, outside in the village. Overgrown with pine greens and snow whites, spruce galore but no dandelions, these are Gutenberg whites.

Old doors flung open by a frosty wind and cold that bites the soul.

The wolf has fur, it protects itself.

And he's hungry. You recognise his hungry look. You also confirm that it's not a wolf but a she-wolf, which complicates the thing over three degrees warmer.

Which warms you by fear.

You cling to the rifle even though you know there's nothing to do but beat each other to death.

Wolf meat, a unique delicacy.

In a burning fire.

For one night you may eat.
If you're not eaten.

Doors slamming in the wind, outside. So does yours.

The wolf is distracted and goes to see what it is – front door, you by the window, with that long, dirty rough beard of yours; breathing no longer vaporises. The heat inside the house is no more, freezing with death, a breath through a fireplace begging for wood.

Doors slamming.

The she-wolf turns around again and looks at you – you know she saw you! - you met eyes in the eyes and now yes, soon you'll know who the real predator is – at every second tension rises, in a deafening heartbeat – if only the she-wolf couldn't hear your heartbeat…

No.

She sniffs all the fear that transpires from your pores and your wrinkled skin – a feast, it'll be – an eye for an eye, no teeth left.

The wind beats on the wolf's fur, undecided.

Concerned.

Worrisome.
You adjust the rifle, eyes in the eyes.
Mistake?
Bullying.

Clenched fists, who wins?
Both looking at each other; *to be analysed*.

Both sharing that exact same instinct at this point – of fifty-fifty, make or break it but, ultimately, both in need of an ally – too many winters alone.

In the end, the she-wolf enters the house and approaches with a step, shy but inspired, and with this naive look.

As if though saying, 'Hi… I'm the wolf.'

And then a recital howls at you.
One of clan…

1

POSTCARDS OF TIME

PAINTING THE PAST WITH B DE BITCH
ODE TO THE EUROPEAN CITY

A SENSUAL, DELICATE and curved shoulder.

'From left to right, please – follow that curve of the shoulder, calmly but decisive and intriguing.'

Helmet-shaped, golden-rouge hairstyle, flying from time to time with the wind; she puffing on a cigarette. Stylish 60's sunglasses, wide on her face, smoke hovering through the air.

Outside.

Day. City. Sunset, yellow-green and greyish tones over the skies – an urban, public garden.

Naked inside and covered only by a man's raincoat down to her mid-thighs, barefoot.

Nothing, without removing it, moves. Only her, nature, the wind and a humming bird over the few trees in the background – whatever comes has to be natural: a fuck by the moonlight!

Studios 2 and 4 shutting down.

'Bosco?'

'Yes, Peter?'

'I'll walk you home – I have my camera, do we film the streets today?'

Pause.

Ash. Ashtray.

Light another.

'Restaurant? My treat,' offers Peter and again.

Walking with Peter, the cameraman – why not? What will it be like to see what Peter sees from his camera? From what point of view does Peter understand what it is to see?

From Peter's, Bosco recalls, urban lines and contrasts are always to be expected on his little gems; close-ups and jump-cuts – sacred moments, even – in a recap of the old masterly retrospective – Fashion, a playful parody!

Movement, wave, cadence.

That makes me move or stop, and then stop too.

That makes me think.

Let it take me, Bosco anticipates, and all this in a very urban way, Peter's filming – but the question remains: with or without a mask?

No... indeed, Bosco still doesn't really know what to say, sitting there in front of the camera.

PAVED, COBBLED STREETS in old stone – nowadays metro station – 'Junk-food and cobbler don't mix.' says Bosco.

Hammer and computer don't mix, said by someone else, coming from the hustle and bustle that accompanies them now through the city, to the beat of honking *a la* mad taxi drivers.

As of old.

'We really fucked up everything.'

'What do you film, Peter?'

'What we fucked up and what we have left – for how long, I don't know.' says Peter.

'What is art for you, Peter?'

'Art? She appears from a corner, always naked, dressed only in a man's raincoat, looking at us.'

'Yes… but nobody remembers the name of the violinist in the string section of London's Philharmonic Orchestra, do they?' she says, before turning a corner again, drifting out of sight.

Art is fearless.

'The artist – the artist is art." says Bosco.

'Performance is art.' completes Peter, panning the camera over the square they now had just cornered, focusing on an ancient statue-foot; voice and body an instrument, as important as any other.

'That instrument becomes a linguistic vehicle.' Something that is sometimes not possible to convey in words.

'The instrument becomes a mean of communicating sensations – of a certain energy.'

'And it has to be respected.'

'Always!' says Peter.

'For every problem, we keep selling the solution.'

'We really fucked up everything…'

SEARCHING THROUGH HER thoughts and in complete silence, *she* always watches you through the window of her gaze – always!

Four words demanding solution, enigmatic in its essence but never definitive – like a simple digression.

Or a postcard from a time soon to be timeless.

That claims logic.

'Will you come back to me?'

Is it over there?

She'd spent the day walking downtown, until she decided to walk back home, absorbed in everything that could be extracted from a four-word riddle:

Allegory, Fable, Mystery or Symbol

'A PORTRAIT OF SOCIETY or just pure waste of time?' she asks herself.

Vanna, housemate, bed mate and endless confidant, was away for a few days, leaving her with their rented apartment at her disposal. Allowing her to avoid, too, and thus the regular use of that bright - *over-the-top* - chandelier, hanging in the living room like a Louis XIV so bright she could not stand – a white, psychiatric ward! A small oak table-lamp was just enough, just perfect, emitting a much more soothing, ochre-dim light.

Warming her soul.

For *her*, it all comes down to Feng Shui, though we used to call it just harmony.

Even in chaos.

Especially in chaos.

Quickly organising and reorganising concepts? – a mandatory night routine. Only then can she take that much-desired bath and forget – to forget – but never without remembering – each and every time, 'As she undresses, gently, camera 2...' – how much she longs for a sign:

A man's raincoat falling off her shoulders, her feet cooling down on the cold bathroom floor – naked and beautiful, *she* sees herself in the mirror, now getting ready to wash the make-up off the day.

Or vice versa.

Thinking.

In so many things and at the same time.

About two strange characters, seen about twenty minutes earlier, on her way back home.

'Spell or charm, not everyone sees art.' had said one of them, plump but with this noble, friendly allure - and the camera says it all.

Spell or charm, not everyone sees art.

'But the camera says it all!' *she* says, emphatically and to the mirror!

Perhaps the only one unaware of it, arched by a pair of light eyebrows lives a candid pair of crystal-blue eyes, reflecting on that mirror.

Delicate rosebud of an ear and a *tout-petit* nose, proportionately sculpted to perfection, some would say, creating, in all its complexity and even from an early age, this portrait of an almost angelical figure, kind and guiding – extremely beautiful yet of a certain maturity.

What makes it angelical?

Maturing of life.

Nowadays reaching sweet-point.

A warm light from the side of the mirror accentuating an even more pronounced shadow to her high cheekbones – which she plays with; above and below, to the sides, gently rotating her face, shading also two delicate, kissable rosy lips.

Through her smile, that adorable smile everyone sees except her—hides an oyster white with a delicate undertone, behind where also and indefinitely lives Lady Insecure.

Always!

Art plays on insecure gains – on a tightrope – sometimes finding itself in the insecurity of a smile. Almost polished to perfection, *she* will never fully interpret the fascination she carries with her as something beautiful.

Never!

Art says something and that's it.

Taking a deep breath as she fills her lungs with air, two erect nipples point even further than normal and in opposite directions.

'Hey there, East-West...' she says, satirically, as she gets inside the bathtub. She knows she has two very generous breasts.

'Focus on all the beauty of a breast, camera 1, passing by, without slowing down... without neither modesty nor prejudice, I want grain in that image. I want to feel the same shiver she feels when she undresses, there, explained by a breast.'

And it didn't take long before she adjusted the water a tad warmer, as she approached it under the shower. Resting her shoulders against the cold mosaic walls and in contrast, as if though purifying the day, art feels.

A bombardment of feelings from a hot thirst.

Emotions she cannot distinguish, rising from that same flow of daily events, now shared with what makes her purest, deeply-felt lifetime thoughts, assumptions, et all what *she* is.

Gently allowing that stream of hot water to run down and through her hair, behind her ears, finally into every pore of her face – by the time that water-jet hit the surface of her shoulders, shivers of pleasure ran down her spine – 'Feeling, camera 1, every drop of water counts!'

As her nipples harden thickly with joy and pleasure.

As water runs down and around her breasts, gently and down.

Down and following the avenues of her body.

Around navel bliss.

Behind, through her buttocks.

And before the quickest of drops came to flood her pelvic region, five elegant fingers were already caressing each other and for a while, around and around.

Squeezing and at the same time that pair of magnificent breasts she'd been bestowed with, with fervour and passion, art masturbates in a cocktail of infinite possibilities.

NOW LET'S LOOK AT IT from an ironic point of view. Let's imagine the stereotype of the being, the only true measure of comparison between peoples: the secular, mundane and profane result, *see tens of centuries*, where perception of a foreign people sometimes comes as forced adoption, not always desired.

And here we are.

Imagine any case, at random – that of the Swiss or the Japanese, perhaps, or the South American or even one of those African countries we can never identify on the map: the thought that comes next - everything your excellency may find in the meridian pocket inside that brain of yours - is nothing more than a step-by-step climbing of that great staircase which constitutes individual evolution itself; the guy who does nothing more than wank his whole life runs a serious risk of not understanding jack shit of what's going on around him.

On the other hand, whoever travels, observes, stays and uses rational tact as form of inter-social initiation - this one, yes, is in serious risk of coming to know the true flavour of what melting the soul of a nation means.

And we are few.

We arrived at the sweet-point of intersocial saturation – the fuck you come here and tell me how things work round here! – fuck it, this is ready to explode.

We can all sense it...

We've entered the next phase of the Global Civil War of the 20s, in early 21st Century.

Smart phone ready?

2

SILENCE OF SNOW

... FORMER PRAGUE LEFT behind, nowadays submerged in the abysmal decline of an obsolete past, Luigi Bosco and the she-wolf continue their journey, towards the south and over an Europe entirely covered by snow; high, low, dry or powdery, by now both grand masters in recognizing the crystallization of snow a week ahead.

Empty rifle always at hand, *just because*, and Bosco had never thought he'd receive so much from his traveling partner. Moreover, all this time without ever finding it strange; something truly intersocial had occurred in the relationship between the two: when one ate, both did, down to the smallest crumb of stale bread.

They supported each other.

How a wolf can perceive a man and vice versa is for God to explain, if he deigns, one day, to speak to us concretely, without fables, analogies or false pretexts - a simple red card will do.

And two yellows always mean shower.

But from the nearest clan, rumours are heard, it seems it will melt. We had two days in a row of less cold. Because it was less cold... Hope resides and persists in the fine line of the bitter taste of having to survive. And nobody gave in. Crises, wars, extinction in sight over and over and even then, humans didn't unite, thinks Bosco.

Looking at the she-wolf beside him.

Caressing her with a friend's hand. Two years had passed and Bosco had never chosen to tame her – the same door you came is the exit one, you can go whenever you want.

And she'd stayed - amazing!

We killed a few who attacked us.

We survived.

We ate venison, fish, rubber – whatever we could find.

Nights are cold. A planet, stubbornly deciding not to melt for decades.

It was in plain sight and no one saw it.

Typical...

... Unexpectedly, a stone-throw away down the valley, three loud drunken *gorillas* from a nearby clan - armed to their teeth!

The she-wolf, spiking up her fur, heard them and beckoned - Bosco slowly asking for calmness with one hand, which she understands.

The *gorillas*, up through that snow like three troglodytes, ready for shit, Bosco sensed, now crouching.

The she-wolf takes cover in the snow, imitating Bosco but there's nothing to be done - one of them seems to see Bosco and it'll be death or glory! To flank, what both trained for two years without being asked, telepathic, instead and again – as the she-wolf takes a few yards in quick steps to the right and on the lookout - Bosco mirroring the movement symmetrically, but to the left, whilst squatting.

Bosco's old army knife, only weapon truly said and well adjusted, within reach and ready to bury itself in three less gorges in this world; three finger blood-prints to be added to the leather-belt he wears - as sign of respect, circumstance or even ritual, while, the wolf in turn, well... her sharp teeth drooled with suspense.

The first one who saw him stops, shotgun in his hands and, from half drunkenly laughter there was total silence.

The silence of a windless snow. The muffle of condensed air increasing with each step and sound, as if a microphone had been strapped to their boots, but in a soft snow, today - without crystallizing or scraping – a soft crackling, difficult to hear from afar.

In the middle of the day where, between sky and ground, there was no more than a blend of this almost indistinguishably white.

Smoothly, Bosco hides behind a tree.

And then another, and another one after that, down the valley - the sound of Wolfy lost in the wind – but the two well synchronized, as attacking wingers and nevertheless.

While the three *gorillas* kept mounting up the valley, in straight line – not realizing they were actually being outflanked.

The five advancing with their blood flowing! Three vandals, Bosco and a she-wolf, synchronized in a single thought - cynical yet honest: to continue or to die, that is out Shakespearean question for the contemporaries.

This when Atlantic, Indian and every single Ocean on Earth finds itself frozen - topped by layers and layers of gigantic sheets of ice - to the point where even the most fearless of huskies asks himself the same question twice:

To cross it or not to stay?

Approaching, finally, in the blink of an eye, the action unfolds. Incredible how a wolf always knows its role, that of main or supporting actor - countless times when one saved the other and vice versa -, when, in a leap from out of nowhere, Bosco's knife came to nail in the throat of the ring-leader with all its might and weight! Half-a-hundred years, to be precise, buried down on that neck - jumps as it rips, skin and death splashing all over! The remaining two hesitating between shock and spasm, but without any time for regrets - because Bosco kneels down on one knee, as if though laying down his weapon on the ground, conceding - but the blade continues, instead, swiftly lodging itself in the windpipe of the nearest one – take that, Zorro!

Finally, and trapped by the wolf, it didn't take long for the third and last one to spit blood too in free fall; neck, lips, torn hair – it was a wild scene that of a wolf's teeth lacerating skin and bone without forgiveness.

Culminating in howls of victory. Panting and completely splattered with alien blood, what does it mean to be from somewhere these days, Bosco thinks?

When an orange sunset decides to occur in his mind.~

A very hot, bursting memory over the whole region.

All this Bosco sees, there, blade in hand...

... Vineyards and olive groves in abundance and excellence, a scorching blessing that are the summers in his unique Mediterranean.

Oh Summer...

'I didn't see you arrive.' *she* says, entering through the kitchen; still carrying grains of sand in between her toes.

Rustic doors on an open Tuscany, with inviting terraces; peaches, good fish and Vermentino Bianco set on a table, high-quality sausages and fresh cheeses, all this when a hot air shades Bosco's terrace in the latter part of the day, before a lazy sunset.

'Come September, I'll write.' says Bosco.

A pause flies over their eyes, half closed due to that great, main lamp that is God Sun, even in the shade; in those kinds of summers where garlic smells and tastes like garlic. Dried oregano arrives as a perfume that calls, attracts, falls in love, something unheard of in Nordic lands, it doesn't exist – only fuck, really, no romance.

'A close-up shot of them two, please – first shivers of an announcing evening, the two kissing without worries.'

Without thinking about time, which had stopped – and which will not return.

That time which, divided, could find you at this very moment at half of your final stretch – tick-tock, tick-tock - maybe you only have half a life left to live, who knows?

Memories of a special shadow, seen and felt only by a kiss.

And the touch of a hard breast on his dry lips, on a hot day. All this assimilated Luigi Bosco, in contrasts of splashed blood, there, in perfect arcs and in the snow.

On his beard.

Embedded in the sweaty clothes he'd been wearing for eternity, it seemed: a heavy bearskin coat covering it all, washable only by time.

How did we get here?

Swiping blood from a blade.

Memories of touch.

They're fingers that touch, lightly –hands that intertwine, squeezing each other in the blink of an eye, contemporary but lasting.

Something natural, it was begged, in a muted world which screams, loudly, yet deaf and artificial. That human touch we've lost and felt at a global, macro, economic and, finally, without delay, anti-social levels.

Running away from touch, we found ourselves.

Running away from the olive tree and the mountain.

Mountain which, on the other side, is no longer a mountain, it has died.

Abandoned.

Everything more and more synthetic.

And more.

And more, we always wanted more.

Agonizing and saturated, 'Uninterested people always become uninteresting.' says Bosco to the she-wolf in the pool of blood around them.

This one of coagulating reds.

'BLACK AND WHITE, CAMERA view divided in half, symmetrically and suddenly, camera 3!'

Seen from above and panning away, it could even be two roundabouts, but no – a close-up of two thick, generous nipples, instead, with no camera perspective at all – two-dimension only, circular – on a reverse close-up that moves slowly away.

Slowly.

'Rather slowly, here - one takes a breather - the story breathes for a while; give them time to soak up all that blood.'

All thanks to a feminine breathing that moves away, seen only by the camera. The camera, the viewer and the voyeur of times - but how long it takes for a lung to fill and deflate – 'All that in crescendo, *Maestro!*'

Which then swiftly transitions to negative.

Positive.

Negative again and again positive, always growing, slide and now yes! with time and distance, those two nipples finally look like two perfect roundabouts, quite explicit on the large screen.

'As perfect as Giotto's O! – like two wide-open eyes the colour of shadow and over a colourless sea - just light, in the contrasting white that paints those two breasts... very Bauhaus, always moving away, very slowly.'

'Very close-up – I want to breathe when *she* breathes...'

I want to hear *her* breathing, which comes to us later, very softly... accompanied by a cello, in low notes, far away.

Lasting; of underground or under-the-bridge acoustics, reverberating in the soul, yet slowly increasing. On and on and on and on, to the point of suffocating, 'Filmmaker, actor, but above all art director – can you fucking hear me?!'

Can you convey all this to the character before *Action* is even heard?

While Bosco looks at a whitish horizon of eternal winters, down there, in the valley; perplexed, knife in hand, his breathing still steaming with death.

'From the first scene, with Bosco sitting on his program – not knowing what to say in front of the camera, stuck in the meshes of being, etc., and going on out there; around the city, rambling about Art, Woman and portraying *time* - the transition to a very cold, icy future - can you show all that without saying it in a scene?'

On a paragraph?

Nothing and no one replaces the value of the scene director, as far as scenes are concerned.

As nothing and no one replaces the director for an actor, when talking about characters, 'Because film is the residue of a mixture of values, aesthetic and symbolic, glued to a make-believe of movements, lines, light and sound.'

Or the abstention from it, this is how emotions are created - in the shadow of a breast!

On the facade of a building, in a city, in the middle of the night - a bed, screwed up to a wall, up on a fifth floor and protruding, literally, as in your bedroom.

Bedside-table plus lit lamp and everything - imagine waking up thirsty in the middle of the night: you get out of bed and fall off a fifth floor!

What do you feel right now, there, falling?

Saved in the nick of time by a musical note! A loose, wide-ranging, low-pitched echo from a cello, three times your size, which catches you in the air and flies, high, high, high in the sky!

You cling to the thick strings of that same giant cello which, in desperation and in turn, depends on pegs and volutes but, snail-shaped and fearless, this may well be the musical note that varnishes, mercilessly, that final note of your possible end.

A musical note coming from the winds.

'Yes, cello-playing in the wind, damn it! - vibration, volume, cameras 1, 2, 3 and 4 - always following!'

Always switching between shots – sound and image in tune, in this great symphony that is life!

Grave and strident notes flying, with you and carving up ghosts in the skies, alas made up only of your own demise; they are the voices that shatter through the turmoil of clouds and mists, from the top of the night, addressing you.

Heading to the moon.

You go to the moon and what do you feel, hears Bosco, but it's his inner voice; and that's when he realizes the reflection of the she-wolf from the corner of his eyes, in the blade of his knife.

She seemed busy, lost in the lickings of a bloody glory.

SHE, naked and lying on her side, in the sun, on Bosco's terrace - where ten fingers run softly over your body like on a piano, playing a sweet melody.

In the shadow of a breast.

3
THE TRAP

You come home tired, at the end of the day.

The therapeutic taste of not knowing what comes next, that you seek and that you receive, your Majesty, here and now - for that is my name: Extempore, the readjustment of your soul, less and less existing.

More and more necessary.

You enter your house, tired from another day.

You want success.

Reset.

You release your feet off the high-heels and let out a sigh. Inert for a long and counted sixty seconds without thinking about anything, you lean against the wall.

You fall into the first trap - that of wanting to go back and open your eyes but you fight it, and count. Eyes closed, twenty-one, and two, twenty-three, and four...

And five, and six, in cadence.

Sixty seconds of nothing.

Black or dark, what you see doesn't matter, let it go, let it flow, and count... thirty-seven, and eight, and nine.

You breathe.

Background.

Taking a step forward, you lean against the bookshelf in your living room and you take a deep breath again.

Looking for nothing.

From where serene odours of manila-hemp flood you with pleasure - you running two fingers lightly over the bookshelf. Maybe your nothing has music, maybe it comes in silence, but you follow it without protest.

Forty...

Fifty.

You open your eyes, and let your hair down.

You slide down the sofa, effortlessly:

Cocteau Twins' *Lorelei*.

'IN SHORT, THE BIGGEST problem of the last century was that of wanting to indoctrinate a left-handed until he writes with his right,' says Bosco, but neither him nor Peter can look straight anymore. This at three in the morning, down the street - drunk as a bunch.

Cocteau Twins' *Lorelei's* singing loudly from a smart phone, 'Re-educating him, demoting him, to nothing more than excrement most of the time... a societal error – parasite!'

'The one from the 21st century, instead...' unexpectedly unleashes Peter and out of nowhere, showing a great deal of alcoholic resilience, '... lies in wanting to solve everything with one stroke...'

'... but both make the eternal mistake of not learning from the past... like redfish in soft waters.' says Bosco, looking at the cameraman and meanwhile.

'Or a Sardinian cheese fondue...' completes Peter, belching; spitting out an arc of vomit, '... we're literally witnessing the long funeral of creativity.'

'Without autopsy, only critic remains...'

'No art, just greed and criticism!' yells Peter, camera rolling again and out in the night, now in circles.

'Nobody remembers Diderot and the likes anymore, or the endless variables culminating in real revolutions – with rotten tomatoes; where popular fairs gave way to authentic public beheading festivals!' says Bosco, finally, in front of a camera!

'Et vive la France!' shout the two of them, loud in the night.

IN THE SHADOW OF A protruding breast, in a sea of love, you make love and lose yourself from everything.

Out of the blue.

Maybe your nothing has music, maybe everything comes in silence, but you follow it without protesting, now to a frenetic *Ocean, O Sun,* by Jason Kao Hwang.

Upside down, there, on the sofa in your living room, you are *She* and *She* is you at the same time - you abstract yourself from yourself, or yourself and see yourself again: sometimes idiot, sometimes a good guy.

You admit it.

To abstract from oneself is the admitted relationship, without blinders, in the eyes of the big mirror, like Pandora's box, something one does not want to open at any time.

Abstracting yourself reveals secrets.

Of those sacrosanct.

Paradoxically, abstracting reveals.

And you feel tired.

... When, suddenly, in the tiniest split-second, a deep pulsation is heard throughout the entire world...

Of unimaginable magnitude – never heard before!

Pam!-Pam!

... Coming from the bottom of the heart of our planet, deep down it pulsed and everything stopped...

... In the city, in the countryside, over the lands and under the seas, seconds later followed this tectonic, crimped crash - no more than a simple bang -, and everything crumbled around us, falling apart...

... What will become of my son, you hear Bosco say, seconds later, there, naked on his Tuscan terrace and in the sun.

'Son, grandson, great-grandson, what will become of them in the future?'

4

RIVER FLOW

'Bosco!' he says, invited to enter the cold house in large steps; shy and like someone carrying a wolf in his arms – this latter wounded and a sad one, paws dripping blood.

'Sara.' Says the delicate voice, with a French accent, 'Come in, please... ugly wound, it seems – *ou-lala*, here, quickly! – let's warm her up by the fireplace while I get some medicine.'

'Thank you, Sara...' almost didn't even notice to say Paolo, Luigi Bosco's great-grandson and heartbroken; by his friend, who seemed to be fighting for her last heartbeat, thinking, this one was tough.

Howls the she-wolf, or tries, in a painful, tear-eyed yelp; in blood, but something or someone who protects me, she seems to think.

'Hold on - without you I'm nobody!' says Bosco, looking her straight in the eyes.

Sara hears him, from the back, hesitating.

Watching Paolo Bosco, who had never felt this way about anything or anyone, there by the fire: the true meaning of unconditional love - no asking, just giving and giving.

'Hold on tight, please...'

EXPLAINED, THE POLES attracted each other and the planet tilted.

In a jump, it spun on its axis and this in a nanosecond; this thunderous, magnetic pumping of gigantic dimensions - a deep, deep carcass-like wreckage-sound from the depths of Earth, heartfelt and which, with it, took us all in to somersault.

To this day, no one has been able to explain the feeling – but something has changed.

Forever.

A magnetic grief that encompassed us all to the depths of soul, bone and flesh – our brains still readjusting; from winter to winter, in a millisecond and so it was, stagnating in what seems to be our eternal epilogue: It had moved of an inch, Mother Earth, from its orbit, and it was total stampede!

'SIDES ARE BEING CHOSEN...' Sara says, sadly apprehensive whilst coating the wolf's torso with bandages and medicinal herbs; this one struggling, wanting to recover.

'... But everything binary - make or break it, all or nothing - the black or white of an eternal yes or no, without ever but never remembering that maybe, just maybe...'

'As soon as Wolfy recovers, we'll start going.' says Bosco, after a moment and by the window.

Night.

Candle light.

A casserole of salt and water.

'We can run away, but for how long?' asks Sara, thirty-six winters well fitted, and considering, brunette and with the cutest freckles embellishing a petite et belle face.

'Until God Sun returns.'

'Sometimes...' Sara almost whispers, caressing the wolf, who now tries for a sporadic breath of hope; of some soft contour. '... sometimes I just want to crawl back in time... to my mother's womb...'

And sleep...

ABOUT A FEW SECONDS it seemed.

However, from Tokyo to Bangkok, New York to Seville, in straight, oblique lines, everything fell in to pieces – or more like crumbling ashes, no monument escaped.

Control towers and skyscrapers, ten-thousand or more years of a once giant world sinking into ruins, as cracks opened in the planet's crust. Followed by colossal sharp spikes that rose out of nowhere – these were all the forests of the world spearheading at you, vast portions of land dissipating itself, turning to precipices.

About seconds it seemed, no one knows for sure but, in a thin at first but unforgiving way then, then followed the biggest flood ever, sweeping everything away – monsoons a laugh, in retrospect, and all flooded away.

For months.

'There are those who travelled between continents on top of rooftops in only a few hours!' people told, such were the currents: a torrential orchestral tragedy, with yours and my name engraved for any anthropologist to drool over in a future, looking into our past.

Rediscovering oneself - sowing, a whim, alas.

With no time to contact either family or friends, so it was – kids at school sailing out there on an endless goodbye. Goodbye son, that's how the salt in your mouth tasted, coming from the corner of the tear that ran down your face, such was the silence in the soul: 'Goodbye, son...' was heard.

For months.

We cried.

On a piano beat of a single note under your skin, like on a Brian de Palma's - that's how the night had passed, at Sara's house: between not knowing if one would still exist by dawn.

War-drums thumped all night.

Trumpets of clans.

Of future honourable men and good farms. That of future peoples who will follow them, unintentionally, willingly or without even knowing it.

The useful votes.

Men and women who've drawn swords through this snow for decades, while the wolf lulls; somewhere between holy sleep and final absolution - but this one's a hard nut to crack; half-asleep. in the middle of the night, Bosco sees her approaching. She then lies down beside him and a ray of hope invades his soul - by rocket!

'Sara!' He wakes her, both still slumbering on her old couch, 'Does the old wagon out there still run?'

'And who's carrying her?' Asks Sara, scared and in that sensual accent of hers, French and when, loudly, a gunshot is heard throughout the night!

'The two of us!' Bosco intervenes, whispering. 'We'll carry Wolfy in the wagon, if we have to - but we have to get moving!'

Hollow and cold, amid screams of hate, conquest and torch-burning revenge ever so near, Bosco, Sara and the she-wolf set off on their way in the early hours of the morning. Down the mountain, dragging the cart under a moonless, sunless darkness; a snow too slow to melt for more than thirty years by now. Solstices no longer celebrated, devoured instead.

Machete and hatchet, two scythes for long distances, if necessary - three shotguns, six bullets plus knife, so Sara and Bosco provided themselves, running down the mountain.

Getting bogged down in the snow.

It wasn't going well, the initial plan.

Even when, and this knowing that, staying would mean death.

Drops the wagon!

Shotgun steady and ready for that fatal kick, as voices are heard closer and closer!

Torch-light invading the immediate darkness, through the trees - dozens of heads, at least, assumes Bosco, this is the fate that follows him.

'Sara, hide!' Bosco tells her, squatting down, leaning his forehead against hers, both hands on the shotgun and busy – but eyes in the eyes. Sara kisses him!

She kisses him but not without letting a stream of tears run down her cheeks.

Piano.

Sad piano.

'I want a sad piano note.' Tears of death, Sara cries, and of survival, as she looks at Wolfy, lying in the wagon, wanting to recover.

Shotgun ready, but there's no time for more, as the first one jumps off from their backs! No more than enough time to take aim, swallow and burst the horns of the lord that follows! - one by one, bullet by bullet, until all was left was crushing skulls into a pulp as solution - there were about a dozen casualties caused in the dark of night.

In the dark of snow.

Twelve fell.

Until one caught him, from behind, in a squirt of infernal pain, but something had just pierced Bosco's back, who kneels, fallen.

Followed by a valiant blow on the head that knocks him down!

AND WAKING UP DIDN'T come sweet at all, because, later on, Bosco realizes the authentic carnal festival unfolding before his eyes:

They were about seven of them raping Sara, without forgiveness - she on a leash, tied to a tree, with her legs wide open, scraping butt in the snow.

Which scratched her at every blow without forgiveness, Bosco without strengths to get up, although he tries, in vain.

Something he says, in vain, too.

Words without a sound.

Tears of impotent pain.

Drying on the face.

Sarah suffering. Dumb-suffering, inert and defeated, in a certain way, while being relentlessly penetrated in the dead of the night.

5

DAWN

'A VIOLIN BOW RUBBING on an amplified electric guitar, please, but softly, softly...'

Bosco gets up, or tries to, when this excruciating pain stretches his skull!

'Sara?!' Bosco releases, in immense pain, startled and looking around:

Dawn.

Icy.

Silence.

All eternally purplish blue. But, in front of him, and dug in the ground, Bosco notices that the wolf had actually dug what appeared to be some kind of alcove.

Dragging her by the teeth, he knew well and guessing, the Wolfy had eventually saved Sara from certain freezing death, wrapping herself around the naked, wounded body of the fragile holy-soul who'd saved her.

But when he tried to move, from Bosco's back all he got was blood and pain, in a hundred rabid-dogs cursed-like fuck!

Crawling, whilst clinging to the wound, Paolo Bosco takes a long minute to get closer to Sara, only three meters away and curled up in the sanctuary that was the she-wolf.

Where her dry eyelashes try to open from the wounds, notices Bosco, halfway through. 'Calm down, Sara.' Bosco tells her, 'Calm down...'

Finally curling up in the alcove as well, both Sara and the she-wolf receive the warmth of his heavy, bloody bearskin-coat, which comes to rest on their bodies. In fact, the three of them fit well inside, tightly curled up – the wolf noticing the gesture.

Managing, but not without monumental effort, to hug both Sara and the wolf inside, Bosco thanks her, with an eternal, 'Thanks, Wolfy...'

Which Sara hears, peeling off an eye.

Bosco caressed his friends for a long time.

So had the clan left them, like that, given to their deaths; no doubt continuing the onslaught down the mountain, thought Bosco, once his brain started to do maths.

In the cold morning, one more, but as soon as the wolf had confirmed Bosco as capable of defending himself, she delicately released herself from inside the heavy coat.

Leaving the two humans alone and hugging each other, as one of the three had to think about the next step: that of hunting something, surviving and keep going.

While you, you and I think.

We run away from a reality created by none other than ourselves, plus the thousand-one gazes of others, ready to burst on our trunks – we know that something has to change, but we are no longer there.

Just like Bosco.

We were what we were and we are no longer. We no longer believe in anything or anyone. We've gone a thousand times over the same subject but, after squeezing, only pus comes out.

Think.

Everything reeks of corruption.

And it tastes like poison.

It flows like a drug through your veins - surreal, because it no longer touches the real, it's fake.

Everything virtual, fake and viral, it is no longer the world we were born in, but we are part of it - we had our opportunity on Earth, but we only thought of the after Earth, greedily.

You cover your eyes like a donkey and swear you'll be forgiven, up there, when you're advised a second way.

A second life, you say, but not without letting out an ironic smile, full of sarcasm and recognition - we screwed up big time, everything we could on Earth, and now you want a second life? Make no mistakes, there are no second lives, Johnny, it was really here that you should have been good, supportive and et cetera.

And et cetera, in an et cetera without dots – very complete, really - you are the sinner who had the blessing of living on planet Offer, as Mother Nature calls it in the ancestral forest:

Home.

Planet that gives, while you take, steal, more, more, more – you always want more!

Suck it, sinner, for the hand that catches you is the hand that bites you, because, up there, there is no forgiveness - be disillusioned.

And spin around yourself, in the middle of your living room as much as you want. Dance with yourself until you lose balance – you want to fall, but in a pure dance, don't ya?

Except that this one comes bittersweet.

You lost your north.

You want to fall. And you dock, luckily - safe or saved by the spiral of rhythm that rocks us, from where you don't want to leave; you don't want to go back, these are interesting conga beats.

'I want to hear even the blink of an eye, now.'

Yours.

You want to be moulded by a soft harp that'll guide you for the rest of your days, but you feel weak and there is no turning back.

You wake up positive for a new day, already saturated and ugly – the ugliest of countenances behind every look on the streets where you live – nine out of ten, and you finally give up.

Waiting for another end of the day.

You hope to be rocked, one day, by a sweet, sweet lullaby of holy harps - without wanting to interpret holiness neither, you just want peace of soul: something that's been taken from you since the day you lost your innocence - you're a part of it, now, welcome! - locker number seven, and yes, the sock-soaking sweat has been there for decades, welcome to our factory: we produce dreams to match your nightmares.

The boss getting fat, laid out in the pool and in the sun.

Aristotle spoke of begging, well before Christ, even questioning the existence of the Gods - Greeks by the way - and because they closed their eyes to such human suffering. And we still haven't managed to abolish it, begging - this is how social backwardness of today's world is measured:

'Camera framing random human faces, out of nowhere and very urban.'

Poor in spirit.

We are made that way.

No forgiveness.

No gold medal at the end of a hard life - suck it, servant, 'cause in the wake of your nightmare I create my dreams - and boy, how good it is to live in a dream!

Feels well.

You?

Who are you, you little shit?

Peace is asked.

With the lightness of a feather, please, and that's what you ask after all this, but who do you call when you make love?

What name do you give to climax?

Do you call it God, or... do you call for God?

You let yourself go, over a violin bowing on a guitar string, reverberating inside that god-forsaken soul of yours. You accept it, you let yourself go, in search of peace.

You try to clear your soul, like an eviction of moments that no longer serve you. You are the bursting box of all your problems – and it is time to empty it.

Problem 1 - cigarette.

Number 2, whores and cigarettes – but... women, do they also see hookers?

It's time to empty that box. Appreciate the fact that, at your core, you are stardust. And that soon you will walk towards the sun, through the air, where nothing disappears, everything transforms.

Cyclically speaking, you shall return.

Maybe in crocodile tears, maybe camel ovaries or sesame seeds, who knows, but it returns.

You're welcome.

You stop and imagine, sitting at your living room table, that same bookcase in front of you – because there has to be a solution for all this shit!

'Otherwise... what the hell is the point of walking here?'

You accept the violin bow that insists on destroying the flame of your being, there, in a broken loop.

That hurts the ears of some, but not yours - not everyone understands art.

You find yourself in those notes, and in the squirt of pain that comes out of the amplifier - why, you don't know -, but without ever giving up. Except that, at this moment, you ask for peace.

Of such lightness that the body glides like a feather, released in the wind.

When the sun shines.

The sun had returned after so long.

The skin warming up, a feeling swept away, somewhere, by worn-out memory.

Unconsciously letting go of that heavy, sweaty garment, Paolo Bosco runs, as though dreaming, over the melting snow and shouting with joy!

Both Sara and Bosco running naked over the meadow, where two thick bushes cover their parts in this sort of Ode to the 70s.

While you, you open your window.

People outside, down on the streets.

Dressed up.

So far everything normal.

Calm down - don't throw fireworks just yet! You know very well you're experiencing what seems to be the rekindling of a flame already dead, of damp wick.

Postcards of time and a postcard you find, on your kitchen table, coffee whistling:

You're Invited To The Biennial Council Of Gods,
Coming From The Gods

You don't understand.

You gave up fighting.

You either accept or don't accept yourself – on a global scale and throughout this society.

And you try to smile.

Until your smile dies, in the middle of the day. You never see it coming, but it kicks and it's gone – something or someone always has to come and shove an avalanche up your ass!

The snowball getting fatter. And you don't even have the patience to dodge it anymore. Invitation from the Gods?

You accept the fight.

You look out the window for excerpts of a flood. Sea levels reaching high mountain peaks.

And certain icons are unforgettable, but you swear that, right in front of you, out there and at cruising speed, the Eiffel Tower passes you, heading towards the mouth of some end.

Of yours, at least, the tower is big, dammit, huge!

Invitation from the Gods?

Why not?

You run down the stairs. And, across the seas of this world, aboard the Eiffel Tower, you are transported or swept into what appears to be a black hole in the sea.

Which you fall in it...

Finding yourself, about minutes later, inside a temple of the Gods, so it seems - everything very dark, with hanging lit torches on pillar here, pillar there.

These are tall pillars, decorated with old art and cuneiform writing, enclosing, down in the centre, an amphitheatre.

You in the middle.

And the echo that it then felt sounded like antiquity.

And no, really, you weren't expecting what came next - a cacophony of sins - all the Gods ever invented, seen or counted, there, useless to number them, they are in the thousands!

Jesus who fights with Jupiter.

Osiris who claims celestial powers.

Shiva, Brahma and Vishnu who look at each other, between the three of them, with a look that says, 'They are fools, these ones.'

Bacchus arrives late, as usual - drunk and euphoric with his antics - poetic songs, arms in arms of Dionysus, twin brother and surprisingly even drunker than Bacchus, now that's' something!

'Behave yourselves, both of you, behave yourself, Bacchus!' orders Mars, but more interested in Venus, from the corner of his eye – who could not give a damn about the session of the Gods, waving a fan.

You in the middle, listening.

Jesus and Buddha a little apart from everything, you feel it.

You see it.

'Behave yourself, goddamn Bacchus - have some decency! - and you, are you taking notes, mere mortal? - this lesson is to be learned!' you hear, from some God that echoes in your soul: the bible of the seven ends, that is the God that echoes in the soul and without room for doubts - something concrete, therein lies the problem:

'Catalogue, catalogue, catalogue!' shouts a certain Euphrates, hands up in the air, coming euphorically at you, surfing a giant wave!

Where the fuck am I?!

You ask yourself, there, in the middle of the amphitheatre; at crossroad number three-thousand and some pocket change, at the pace of that life of yours, aimlessly – without any compass, yet you go.

You always have to go.

Where, you don't know.

You just know you have to go, somewhere, and while you're thinking, in the meantime, it's in that meantime that things get fucked up, usually – when you least expect it. When everything was even going well, it seemed, but something or someone always has to – *oh, fuck it, enough!*

It's no longer enough to say enough.

We crossed that line of enough some time ago now and not even a thinker can save us, because we are all fed up with thinkers. It hurts even baby Jesus, say our distinguished grandparents, these days without a voice but, when the last of the trawlers embarks out in the sea - neither whale nor small fish, every fisherman and every seagull alike will abandon you, you dog, leaving you lost for good in your empty spot.

It's not worth it, you'll hear.

Nothing is, anymore.

We managed to eliminate the value of value, chapeau!

You're the vegetarian ordering salad in a restaurant that sells meat – brilliant! Whether you like it or not, you're an investor of the abattoir.

You are part.

You take sides and choose factions but, right now, making decisions is exactly what you don't want.

You seek a sweet end to this hard chapter; one that heroically sculpts your being, that baggage one carries, it's said, experience.

Because when experience no longer takes you anywhere, my friend, then yes, the world is made of egregious grandparents, you'll recognize and finally.

This world that turned on itself one day, and everything spun around us, remember?

Yes, Bosco doesn't know what to say, there, in front of the camera, it's a fact – the script is to be followed, he knows, except that... and he knows it too well, from re-edited scripts all Gods' advertising is created.

You are part.

You are the instrument of socio-destructive torture - yours, in most cases - you know it well, impotent and inert human robot.

Compare yourself to shit?

You will become shit, then, because your moral compass points there:

You'll be shit all your life.

'And with a smile, please, camera 2 zooming in.'

All this, however, while you think.

While you think, howls the wolf, jumps as it bites and death smiles! Because, when it whirled, and at that apex, dynamite flames flew all over the world, if you think.

The entire arsenal ever seen from every nation in the world exploding, like dominoes, in cadence - one by one relaunching the next, setting it on fire.

Think.

Every tree ignited, before the flood, which followed, moments later.

The smell of ash across the skies, which covered everything next.

Breathing impossible – you grab a handkerchief - this one washed out with acid rain by now, such was the level of uranium in the air.

Think.

Biggest bust ever, globally.

Think.

But now reflect.

Reflect a little.

Reflect on the subject - from thinking there must always come a reflection, or two.

Or three.

In fact, sometimes even more - we need to reflect, because everything goes too fast and too much!

You intend for a happy ending to this story, when, in the end, you are History.

If the future belongs to no one and everyone at the same time, you and I have chosen to leave it in the hands of corrupt politicians; we pay them, moreover, for them to take care of governing – that is our laziness, once measured: Someone other than myself to govern myself. And to think that Theatre and Democracy were born at the same time and in the same place - hand in hand, tragedy and political theatre are our daily bread, that faith.

Faith like a casino, if you think - magic roulette, grant me, consecrate me, make me rich!

So that you can then spit on the poor.

We were made that way.

One-hundred-thousand years of composition, genetically speaking, capable; capable of almost anything, good and evil - we are the species capable of surpassing our physiological limits.

Biological.

Stratospheric and transcendental.

We transcend concepts and leave a trace. We always leave a trace, although, humanely speaking, it's a trace of piss.

Too much.

Too much piss on these streets.

You arrive at the end of the line, jump as you enter, for the train is moving!

Next station: yours and my future - no pressure, it's cool, take it easy - foot on the accelerator, here you always play at home - what can go wrong, right?

Might is right.

Put your foot down on that pedal, but in the opposite direction - fuck my future when yours counts more: because freedom ends when the greed of others speaks louder - here's yours and my world, put your money where your mouth is, says the just, no longer knowing how to define justice.

Search, search, but no longer finds it, in the dictionary, we've taken justice out of dictionaries – you'll find it on an app these days. Especially if it's a serious topic, you are the vassal of the algorithmic passport that carries your blood and mine.

Vaccinated, you are the half-lie that makes up the truth.

And it's true that – surprise, surprise – it's not even in the dictionary anymore, we fucked up big time this time. Dow Jones breaking records, day after day.

While you and I contemplate the doors of bankruptcy, instead, a metallic bang in our ears.

End of the line.

Stop.

Terminal.

Get off the wagon.

Pass the turnstile.

Buy a new ticket.

Board on the next train.

Expected delay of one-hundred-fourteen-minutes or so. Buy that sandwich at the nearest point of sale.

Look at the clock.

Yes, we're talking timing here, one hundred and fourteen minutes is worth one hundred and fourteen minutes.

Multiplied by seconds gives a huge number – better not know it.

Buy that newspaper.

It's not worth it, we have everything at hand, on the smart phone.

Look around yourself, in circles: everything and everyone looking at the screens of a smart phone - don't even think about saying a word to the nearest citizen, he won't shit an answer.

Enter that wagon.

Choose your seat.

Yes, it's time to sit down, but without ever letting go of the goddamn smart phone – a girl is spinning in front, but the boy can't even see her anymore, his horns so glued to the screen.

We are literally witnessing the death of flirting.

It's not worth it, go to the app, you'll find meat for all tastes: busty, blondes, duck-face, the longest dick you've ever seen – all of that at the distance of a finger.

That finger that slides over the screen.

From your smart phone.

It's smart.

You, the donkey that follows it, with your visors well on - go ahead, inert human robot.

Incinerator?

Door 3.

He didn't even see it, glued to his screen.

'Excellent!' says one Mr. Burns.

What a long chapter, this one, that of living. I want to give you a happy ending, but on a sad piano I feel like staying, you see?

Press on the pedal – the piano one, goddamn it! - not the gas pedal!

Stop for a moment, calm the fuck down - this ain't a sprint - it's an endurance test, in reality - calm those horns down, sturdily.

Pretty hard, if you have to.

I really want to leave you a healthy and hopeful ending – but I lack arguments, you know?

Are you still here?

'It means that this one speaks to you,' says Luigi Bosco, in front of the studio camera, 'You recognize yourself, and I thank you... because not everyone sees Art. Beauty and sadness thrown over nuances? It's not for everyone, and if you're still here, I know you know – and a sincere and honest thank you goes your way.'

Bosco didn't make it, in case you're wondering. Neither grandfather nor
great-grandson – all eaten.
Not one got away.

2020

THE YEAR OF FEAR

"FROM WALL STREET TO your street and every street cornering the globe, ripples of doubt keep flying our way on a minute basis through volatile news. Pounding hard on every ding-ding that chimes on every phone we now hold – so smart they are – and ding-ding they go, directly to the back corner of probably every single brain that walks the earth, our earth, that earth that now breathes so freely it sounds too good to be true.

And as the European Markets tank once again by the closing bell over the corona virus, reports from China hail no good winds neither, with warns of more regional lockdowns to occur.

But what are traders really trading, body count?

One thing is for sure, 5, 6% swing moves a day, every day – it takes a strong stomach to swallow those losses.

And what losses, asks the average man and woman who now stands, perhaps, weeks away from household insolvency?

900.000 global coronavirus cases surpassed as I write these words and that is what you're going to read, soon on any news outlet, if you haven't already.

But does this, all this tell another story, I ask?

What is this article about, in the end – in what section should one find it – Economy, Politics, Health and Safety or Business – Sports, maybe?

Yes, as you so rightly presumed, all of those and many more if not all, because unprecedent is what is happening. To the point it got half the world sitting idle on its worries.

And worry we should for every single aspect of our lives is being affected."

- - Article written by the author for The Focus

AND TALK ABOUT THE pile of rubbish we've gone through ever since...

DI FACTO, this one was turning into something a bit too wild. Aware of a dream – know the feeling? Like real, being there, feeling it. A conversation with the past, more like it – but something must be done.

Art has a place, carved on Earth by tribes, and I believe it being a positive one. Art asks. Turns the page. As I do, right now.

Meanwhile,
on the other side of town...

6

SWERVE, PAUSE, HIP

TAKE OFF. FROM EVERYTHING.

Revive, revolve and breathe again, this time without fear.

Back to a recent past, but not that far away. Not anymore. Perspective lost. Lady Perspective has evacuated the building, without giving any news of when she'll return.

Will you come back?

Brain storm. But all I want is to dance. Dancing in the wind and thinking about nothing. I want to stop thinking but without dying – I want to live and I can't anymore. The boat sank to the bottom of an ocean that no longer has a name. And all I want is to fuck.

Feel the touch as he penetrates me inside – a thousand orgasms at once – I want to fuck while we send death to hell and forget about everything.

The everything.

That knock on the door. Let it be him ringing the bell, let it be him going up to my window, getting inside and bumping me up against a wall – rip off skirt and nickers – pick me up and throw me on the kitchen table! - fruit up in the air – books, newspapers, everything up in the air! – let's dance this dance in the wind and send all this shit up in the air!

'With emphasis, damn it!' Shouts Papadilla, the director of the film that will hit the big screen as the most erotic musical ever seen, he swears.

52

'You are beauty with a big B, Julia – Marta, Linna, Matilde, Josephine, you are everything a man wants... when he doesn't have it.'

Ernesto Papadilla. Genius for some, but crazy for most. He doesn't belong, can't be identified – neither with eras nor fashions – all upside down. And he never regrets.

But passing through the hands of Ernesto Papadilla as a dancer, actress or artist is like spinning a thousand pirouettes on itself and somersaulting – twenty-four seven – no time to analyse whether you like it or not – process is learning!

And from what you squeeze, a work of art either comes out or nothing – that's the commitment, like the grape in the vineyard – without signing, contract or promise – it's in his eyes. It's in the way he talks to you and the way he sees you.

In believing, no thongs – stimulated by moment and reaction – yours, if you have it – it's twenty-four seven without forgiveness even when you sleep, how you fuck and that fucks you up.

And no, it's not a requirement or an imperative – it's a mutual decision.

In my case, I never regret it.

'Julia, stop!'

And you stop, in that same position you find yourself – on the tip of a fingernail of a single toe – there you find yourself, curving beauty and there you stay, for a moment.

You look at infinity – or try – in the infinite darkness that is Ernesto Papadilla's rehearsal studio: an improvised stage in an old theatre, remodelled with three strokes of a nail. His way; everything is dark, except for a light, coming from above, which dances in the wind and scalds your skull while you drip, in that moment of pause – as you drink salt dripping from the corner of your eyes.

Which will end in the corner of your lips.

That you lick, when you can, without him seeing it – it's a sweaty tickle, but why the hell does he ask you to stop, you don't know, these are all routine movements for you.

But not for Papadilla.

Because Ernesto Papadilla doesn't see beauty, he sees *your* beauty, unique and different from all others. We are tall, small, blonde, brunette, but not in his eyes, for Papadilla sees sensitivity in a sigh - that whisper sketching your soul all the time – he hears it as well.

And with that, Papadilla never jokes.

It is what characterises being; how to be in this world and who you truly are. Only one condition imposed on the body in which you were born – treat it well and with dignity.

'Ten-minute break, girls... I have to think something, here.'

Papadilla refers to the movement of the wave – or the wave of the movement, I don't know, depending on point of view – but something was missing.

In these moments, we sometimes get the feeling it's not the dancer's fault – it's his. Something had hit him, at a certain point during rehearsal, which made him rethink the whole movement and staging; melody, light, who fucking knows, but at this moment, on that brain travelling at a thousand-miles-an-hour, there's a real brain storm, I know.

As he went, mumbling something like *Postcards of Time* or something.

7

OUR TOILET, PLANET EARTH

THE WORLD WENT MAD those days, they'll say in future generations. How to wash your hands properly, it had started with, before shock and denial paved way to total panic. All that in a matter of days in those early months of 2020 – the entire world focused on one thing only, never seen before, it was chaos!

From Wall Street to your street and every street cornering the globe, ripples of doubt kept flying our way on a minute basis through volatile news.

How to circumvent depression in lock-down?

Six tips for staying active – a blog on how to create another blog during self-imposed isolation – we had mock-ups of an ending civilization on a tag-spree travelling from Brooklyn to Calcutta.

All the while, in economy the markets listened for clues, watching a decade of profits been washed away with massive, unforgiving selloffs.

Pounding hard on every *ding-ding* that chimed on every phone we now hold – *so smart they are -*, and *ding-ding* they go, directly to the back corner of probably every single brain that walks the earth, our earth, that Earth that now breathed so freely it sounded too good to be true.

We could even see the Himalayas in India from a distance and for the first time ever in thirty years!

At the same time, nervous like high-speed race drivers before green light, any day for the trader on Wall Street was a race for survival, those days. The only thing in common with the person on the streets being a sentiment of clueless existence; liquidity depleting and a very strange word which had appeared on Wall Street lexicon in the previous twelve months or so had now hit traders like a two-ton hammer blow:

Idiosyncratic.

Nothing correlated as usual in the markets and there was no safe haven other than King Dollar.

Neither bonds nor gold, there was nowhere to hide and, for days, it stayed like that.

It still is.

That same liquidity which would later fund the recovery was no more – wiped out. Fearmongers, on the other hand, those had been seen growing in abundance and exponentially ever since.

But, on the bright side, this massive selloff was being interpreted as the last ditch-attempt for any type of liquidity possible, in reality – *sell everything you can!* - through desperate dead-cat bouncing days, it seemed, in a term used by markets to describe any leery attempt of a rebound – alas, before buyers give in and sellers take the stage again.

Yes, markets as in... they are an entity, they have a life – they're the trader and the investor behind it.

And all that just before what traders love most, ladies and gentleman – that anticipated slingshot move everyone was waiting for, in the mimicking words of US sitting President at the time, the farting tweet that is or was (he might not be around by the time you read this, who knows?), Mr Donald Trump, with "Stocks will sky-rocket after this pandemic, folks!"

No partisan take here, ladies and gentlemen, I never set a foot in the States.

All the while, in the mundane world, attacks bloomed on social media from all sides and on every language – everyone turned both saint

and expert on Health and Economics, reminding us a wise (normally, let's be fair) Mr John Cleese, who says it clearly on a Youtube video:
"In order to know how good you are at something requires exactly the same skills as it does to be good at that thing in the first place."
Elaborating, Cleese says:

"It means that if you are absolutely no good at something at all, then you lack exactly the skills you need to know that you are absolutely no good at it."

AND, LIKE THAT, CLEESE had given us a brief introduction to the Dunning-Krugger effect – a cognitive bias wherein unskilled individuals suffer from illusory, and so on, etc, yours truly – to put it in the *Pythonesque* style our contemporary epoch deserves.

Furthermore, voicing on how appropriate it was to finally take a peek at that famous study could been seen as an understatement from any humble opinion.

So many questions it raised.

An invisible enemy in the shape of a spreading virus.

And how we'd been living our lives, so carefree of any consequential demise whilst polluting the world on a wave of profit-taking.

Our toilet, Planet Earth.

It begged for global co-operation, the world was shouting, louder than ever, putting into question many if not all that spun around the globe, making 2020 the year of fear.

It led me to question many things myself, as I embarked on a journey of intro-retrospective thoughts. There were so many concepts I could not grasp at the time and, delving into the news or social media was like nosediving into hell – it still is, only exacerbated, try being accurate these days and see where it gets you -, a gigantic pool of finger pointing and theoretical missiles, flying in every direction.

One by one, with every Nation closing its borders.

What then happened was the inevitable sub-sequential action of any domino effect, pushing me to an urge of voicing out even more loosely than I do.

Thoughts which had become unbearable in the indoor regions of my mind. In the parody the world has come to, comedy and philosophy stand as the only sane place to be and, with that being said, ladies and gentlemen, these had to be my monologues.

8

**THE ECONOMIC NIPPLE
(WE ALL SUCK ON)**

IS MONEY THE CAUSE for all good and bad?

We neither eat it or drink it but, instead we're told we need it for all that matters.

And we all suck on it.

Following the reading of an interesting article from my fellow co-worker at the time and editor at The Focus, Alexandra Ciufudean, on **how the world could actually learn from covid-19**, Ciufudean's notes propelled me to the quintessential question of what is it Mankind lives for, in the end – what's this all about? Please allow me to use that capital letter on Mankind – it soulfully deserves it.

We've been trading something for something else ever since we became settlers – forever leaving behind the trading act of hunting for survival (did I just describe Communism as in what is <u>yours</u> is <u>mine</u> and what is <u>mine</u> is <u>mine</u>?), and money can be seen as whatever one accepts as a mean of barter, in order to get something else, be it an object, nutrition or a ticket to Tokyo.

It also used to be a tad more tangible.

COW FOR CORN, GOLD subdivided in silver coins, until a simple sheet of paper became the absolute guarantee of how much someone

59

held on a piggy bank, avoiding the burden of carrying large sums of gold or silver for transaction purposes.

Imagine carrying an elephant.

But it's from observing how Nations are dealing with this pandemic that I come upon some pertinent questions like:

"How can stimulus (future debt) packages help – and why aren't they helping already or, more pertinent even, why weren't they thought of before the "flood"?

Ice ages are cyclical and bound to reoccur so where's the bunker?

How to approach the subject of money these days without sounding too presumptuous or prophetic even, like a guru-bearded man on top of a hill – preaching for change in how we govern, not only this pandemic crisis but the future of Mankind, by skipping all conventional ideologies of the past?

Just for a bit, can we override them, in theory?

Surpass them?

Ignoring them substantially and occasionally, maybe, just for a tiny little bit and just for the empirical sake?

But, bursting, in the end, through the inner core of what life would be without a carrot at the end of the stick, many have tried and many have studied it.

Many have failed too.

In fact, we never stopped doing it so, electing presumed lesser of evils as best options most of the times, worldwide and where permitted – but questions still remain: Would we work and produce for the mere satisfaction and need of doing it so?

No, it's not rhetorical.

Ask an artist or an altruist and the answer will almost be 100 per cent yes but, on the other hand, anyone with a redundant job like a dish-washer or a robot-machine factory monkey might say otherwise.

Something's gone wrong down the road and with inherent damage – something's really wrong in our Society. Something as old as gold itself.

How to govern people's intentions and needs and the limitations of *wanting* without a shared common sense of what the sum of all parts is, as a whole?

Ideology and policy had to come into force because we are, in the end, species of animal instinct, with a forefront leading brain cell's motto saying, *"I want, therefore I take."*

"There's nothing wrong with an arrogant wealth, if you melt the silver yourself."

Luke Haines on *The Upper Classes*, a song back in the 90's from one of the many bands he played in, called *The Auteurs*.

So, how to take?

How many times can I take?

How fair is it to take?

From whom or what am I taking it from?

Evolving as we've always did, a few defining moments in the past 120 years of told history have shaped our existence from an economic view.

And we cannot examine where we are right now without being repeatedly thrown back at Keynes and Hayek – the two colliding economic schools of thought we've all been living according to and ever since.

That much we all agree.

And the winner, evidence might tell, was Keynes.

For the literate in the matter I am but a pupil, trying to learn and one with no hopes of shedding any light on the subject for, I am sure, the same literate in the matter has studied and profited the subject to exhaustion.

But, for the less informed or interested in it, let's say that these two different schools of thought both addressed macroeconomics at a time of recession and depression.

World War I, *Big Depression*, World War II and the culmination in the Bretton Woods Agreement in 1944 (when, finally, a few Nations agreed that some global cooperation had to coexist), that is where

Keynes and Hayek situate, historically and for those who forgot it down the line.

Yes, where we are right now as well, knocking at the door of a global depression and according to many.

Keynes and Hayek addressed on how to circumvent, predict and even avoid economic crisis, shortly put.

Where Keynes said Government should intervene by injecting money and boosting a depleted economy, therefore creating jobs (throughout the *Big Depression* days but his thoughts started way back, in the end of World War I), Hayek opposed, screaming for a *Free Market* to take the lead, allowing economy to fall on its arse, with no Government intervention at all and allowing the *wound* to heal itself for the better good.

As he saw it, Hayek stated that the self-imposed causes were the reason of being there in the first place (referring to economic bubbles inflated by cheap credit which, soon enough, will lead us to the Federal Reserve, Interest Rates and the roles of Central Banks), and they should fall, go bankrupt and allow poverty to take its natural course because, in the end, social Darwin's law of the fittest would resolve.

But did they predict the era of digital money?

BECAUSE, FUNDAMENTALLY, one of the two options will be the outcome in this pandemic – do Governments fund the recovery and sustain the burden of household and corporate insolvencies (through eternal debt) both during and in the aftermath, or do they leave the weak to fall and start all over?

During, in my case, is yet to be seen, though as of the time of these writings – cheers, EU.

Concede me, as well, the power to grant Governments the capital letter-status – they need to be highlighted and, reason being they hold both knife and butter in their hands.

Grounding us to a halt has produced the irrefutable conclusion of how deeply flawed and unsustainable ways we've been conducting our lives, my fellow writer Ciufudean sates and rightly so on her article.

Whilst carelessly ploughing for profit throughout, perhaps, our entire existence – I add here in my own words -, direct or indirectly abetting the crime, we're all left exposed here, with nowhere to hide.

And that, I believe, *has* to be the only point everyone agrees in this pandemic, when we look in the mirror.

As a middle ground for debate, I believe this last statement of mine should be the starting point for any solution-based action taken in the future – because **something has to change at the core** on how to better co-operate, as we live, in a globalized society.

A simple philosophical point might even argue this may well be the cornerstone Mankind so desperately needed, to re-evaluate and even re-interpret the need of money in its essence.

Could this be the laying of that first stone for a future world with no need of money at all?

After all, we have destroyed so many social barriers throughout the centuries – and how Utopian is to foresee a world without money?

Judging history, I'd say money is obviously Mankind's only philosophical tool of guidance for future generations – for where we put our money defines what flourishes as a business and what collapses into bankruptcy.

And is it so that, by taking ruthless competition out of the equation, we, as a species can therefore no longer excel?

AND HERE WE ARE

TAXI FROM JUPITER.

He opens the backdoor of the five-seat Cadillac to much surprise as he encounters an almost empty city. His grandson, popping out with a similar look of awe in his eyes freezes at the sight of a huge advertising board; a smiling man's face caught exuberantly perfect for the camera and a short slogan, mentioning something like *Vote Social-Democratic*, he reads, in big letters.

'What is that, grandpa?'

'Oh, dear... it's an old tradition Man had in the past. Ideology, it was called – political semantics, really - old stuff...'

But how many times do we ask ourselves that grand philosophical question of what's this all about – what's the meaning of life?

Mrs Fletcher, to name one, spent most of her life saying we're nothing but a fiscal number.

They're expecting their third.

It's just wrong.

Ludicrous to plant a third baby in the world if life can be reduced to just another fiscal number.

Should I mingle?

None of your business. Too many opinions. Too many fiscal numbers. Perhaps this is all for a greater good after all and Mrs Fletcher decided to answer that philosophical question with economics. She had a choice and this is what she does.

But how do we manage economy?

POLITICALLY.

In that sense, it won't be too far-fetched deeming Philosophy, Economy and Politics all but one and the same. Or a three-headed derivative of a whole. **We're given economic opportunities from birth, conduct them by the existing rule of law of where we live in, in order to perform our existential purpose on earth.**

But, in that same sense, is it so wrong to criticize market speculators and Wall Street after all? Looking around, what are business made of, even before we look at their product and what they sell?

You enter a shop, where does that counter come from – has some poor, underpaid soul been skimming his or her dreams for a penny so that I can open my shop? That lamp, which *monkey-factory* produced it?

How pious are we in all of this?

If I'd go down the sustainable route full-swing I'd probably stand naked, abdicating of the same clothes I'm wearing right now – the roof of my house, how *eco-friendly* is it and should I care?

How have we been governing all this in reality?

Time stopped and here we are.

A BOOK SITS WAITING on his desk, intended for his grandson, one day.

It was written some 250 years ago by a famous Scottish philosopher on the topic of wealth of nations. It was its title as well. The author, Adam Smith, is considered as the father of modern Economy, we know well – *or modern Economy at that time*, some might add.

But did Smith envisage a world as we have today, guiding us into where we are right now, or did he warned us about it?

Both?

One of the many sold interpretations on that famous essay states that, **in order to have trade between two nations one must have two things: A nation with a sword and another one with debt.**

Brilliant.

Walking around the empty city hand in hand, grandfather and grandson stumble upon a cul-de-sac with an open tavern in the back. It was called *The Arse of Solitude*.

Judging that they might not find anything open for a while, grandfather decided to go in, with sceptical thoughts and scratching his head about the boy's safety.

Yet, thirsty as they were from their long trip – *not many stops between Jupiter and Earth yet -*, he thought no more, and they popped inside.

'Remember, child, they see things differently round here.'

HERBERT SANTORI

Mad Director's Cut
GUTENBERG WHITES
... 50 Years Too Late!

2023

www.ingramcontent.com/pod-product-compliance
Lightning Source LLC
Chambersburg PA
CBHW021749150726
47989CB00004B/1581